Early-to-Read i|t|a Program

Revised Edition

bωk 7

mr. pickl's surpries

Harold J. Tanyzer, Ph.D.
Hofstra University
and
Albert J. Mazurkiewicz, Ed.D.
Lehigh University

Initial Teaching Alphabet Publications, Inc.
New York • London • Toronto

MR. PICKLE'S SURPRISE by Dick and Don Pinnell; BETSY AND THE
MAGIC BOX by Dorothy LaCroix Hill; LOUIS HAS A GOOD IDEA by
Mary Jane Columb; JOHNNY GRAY'S LUCKY DAY by Anne Alexander;
and MR. DOOLEY'S FAVORITE COLOR by Rose-Marie Provencher,
originally appeared in HUMPTY DUMPTY'S MAGAZINE, published in
New York. They have been transposed into the Initial Teaching Alphabet by
the publishers of this book. Copyrighted by the Better Reading Foundation,
Inc. THE PEANUT BUTTER SANDWICH; HOW TO FIND A FRIEND;
LITTLE VIOLET; THE SILVER BIRD EXPRESS; JENNY AND THE SEED;
THE BIG GAME; LARRY AND THE WONDERFUL BOAT; MARTY AND
SMARTY; THE VERY BEST SUMMER are reprinted with permission of the
author, Lillian Moore.

Stories 1-12 illustrated by Eleanor M. Maguire of Design Unlimited
Stories 13-14 illustrated by Victor Lazzaro

The Initial Teaching Alphabet Foundation, an in-
dependent organization chartered as a nonprofit
educational foundation in the State of New York,
certifies that this book uses the characters as
designed by Sir James Pitman and the spelling
rules he developed.

Initial Teaching Alphabet Publications, Inc.

Publishers of Educational Materials in Pitman's Initial Teaching Alphabet

20 East 46 Street, New York City, N.Y. 10017

PRINTED IN THE UNITED STATES OF AMERICA

2-98765432

Contents

1. Mr. Pickl's Surpries   1

2. Betsy and the Magic Box   6

3. Lœis Has a Gœd Idea   14

4. Jonny Gray's Lucky Day   19

5. Mr. Dooley's Favorit Culor   26

6. The Peanut Butter Sandwich   29

7. How to Find a Friend   37

8. Little Violet   43

9. The Silver Bird Express   51

10. Jenny and the Seed   57

11. The Big Game   64

12. Larry and the Wonderful Boat   70

13. Marty and Smarty   77

14. The Very Best Summer   84

Mr. Pickl's Surpries

Mr. Pickl had been janitor of the scool for a long, long tiem. The old janitor luved the children. And aull the children luved him.

One dæ after scool, when aull the children had gon, Mr. Pickl was wurking in the first-græd rœm. A culored pᴇᴇce of pæper under the desk caut his ie. As he picked it up, he red whot was on it.

Birthdæ Party

Lots of cæk

Ice cream

Soda

"A birthdæ party," he said tœ himself. His ies lit up as he thaut of the happy tiems he and the children aulwæs had at these partis. "But," he thaut, "hœm is it for? And it dusn't sæ when it's tœ be." The invitæʃhon wasn't

1

finished. "Well," he thaut as he finished his wurk, "thæ'll tell me aull about it tomorrow when ie get the invitæʃhon."

That niet Mr. Pickl cod hardly sleep for thinking of the birthdæ party and the fun he wod hav helping with the gæms and mæking the children lagh.

Next dæ, no one tauked about the party. At the end of the dæ, Mr. Pickl wæved god-bie to the children as thæ left for home, and still not a wurd had been said about the birthdæ party.

"Well, mæbe tomorrow," he thaut.

But two mor dæs passed and bie Thursdæ afternoon, Mr. Pickl had decieded thær was tω be no party. "O well," he said tω himself, "ie must hav been mistæken about the hole thing." He sieed as he locked the dor tω the scool and went home.

Fridæ morning Mr. Pickl was sweeping the steps as the children began tω cum tω scool. "Gωd morning," he said. But he stopped in surpries as he lωked at the children. For aull the littl girls had on thær prittiest dresses. The bois' shωs wer shiening and thær hær was comed. It was easy tω see that sumthinΩ speſhial was going on.

"ie was riet," Mr. Pickl thaut. "Thæ ar having a party and, for the first tiem, thæ'r leaving me out." The janitor's hart was broken.

aull morning Mr. Pickl wundered whie he hadn't been invieted tω the party. "Well, ie'd just be in the wæ," he thaut. "It will be a better party without me, ie gess." Pωr Mr. Pickl. It seemed the children really had forgotten him.

aull at once the loudspeaker cæm on. "Mr. Pickl, a bottl of ink has been broken in the first-græd classrωm. Bring your mop riet awæ, pleas."

He got his mop and pæl and went tω the first-græd classrωm.

As he cæm intω the rωm, the children wer sitting quieetly at thær desks. Lωking up, Mr. Pickl sau that thær wer pæper chæns of red and yellow and blω that the children had mæd. On the window wer culored pictuers.

Suddenly, the children jumped from thær seats and began too shout, "Happy birthdæ, Mr. Pickl. Surpries! Surpries!"

And a real surpries it was, for Mr. Pickl had forgotten that it was his own birthdæ! "ie thaut you had forgotten too inviet me too your party," he said, "and aull the tiem it was ie hoo had forgotten."

ʃhuer enugh thær was lots of cæk, ice cream and soda, and many wunderfool gifts for Mr. Pickl. Mr. Pickl thaut it was the happiest birthdæ party ever.

*This story originally appeared in HUMPTY DUMPTY'S MAGAZINE, published in New York. It has been transposed into the Initial Teaching Alphabet by the publishers of this book.

Betsy and the Magic Box

At first Betsy didn't miend waiting in the package lien at the post office, but the big peepl did.

They mωoved their packages from one arm tω the uther, and pωt the hevy ones down on the flor.

Everywhere Betsy lωked, there wer packages. Big ones and littl ones. Thin ones and fat ones. Square ones and flat ones. Hundreds of packages.

Betsy tried tω gess whot was in them. But after a whiel she got tiered of gessing.

And her legs got tiered of standing. Tω rest them she stωd first on one fωt, and then on the uther.

"Betsy," sed Muther, "don't hop around liek that!"

"ie hav tω," sed Betsy, "becaus mie legs wont tω sit down. Can ie wait in the car?"

"You wait riet here!" sed Muther.

Betsy sied. Muther didn't wont her tω wait in the car becaus if she lωked too hard at the big Cristmas box in the back seat, she just miet gess whot was in it.

It was long, and wied, and not very hie. Whot cωd it be?

Betsy was trieing tω think when a voice said, "Betsy, wωd you liek tω sit on this?"

The man behiend Muther pωt a square box on the flor.

"It's not a big box," he said, "but it's strong. It has tω go a long way."

"Whot's in it?" asked Betsy.

"Betsy!" said Muther.

Under his dark green hat, the man winked one ie. Then he leaned down and whispered, "It's fωll of magic! There's a taull, black magic hat, and a black magic coat, and a bωk about how tω be a magiʃhan. It's for mie grandsun, Tommy."

Betsy sat down on the box—and jumped riet up again! Becaus the box

shook her just a littl—insied and outsied—
liek a shiver!

"Betsy!" sed Muther. "If you'r going
tω sit on the box, sit still!"

Betsy sat down again and the shiver
was fun.

How cωd a box make you shiver?

Betsy bent over and lωked between
her feet, and she cωd see riet thrω the
box—clear insied!

She cωd see aull the magic things for
Tommy just as plain as if they wer lieing
on the post-office flor, not rapped up at
aull!

She stωd up again and lωked at the
box—it was just a plain box with rieting
on it. So Betsy nue you had tω sit on it.
When you sat on it, it was magic! It let
you see insied things!

She lωked at the man in the green
hat, and he winked again. He nue about
the magic, too!

Insied Muther's packages Betsy sau the spaceman suet for Cusin Dick, and the bok without pictuers for Grandmuther, and the candy for Ant Bet!

The lady in frunt of Muther had three smaull boxes with aprons insied them. A red apron, a green apron, and a whiet apron with a blo hous for a pocket. Betsy had never seen such a buetiful apron.

"Mov the box," sed Muther. "We'r getting closer to the window."

Betsy stod up to mov the box, and aull the packages wer just packages. She codn't see insied any of them.

10

Then she sat down again. And after the shiver she cod see riet throo the rappings, and the boxes, and the Cristmas paper.

She sau a gieant bær! And three shieny pans! Then the lady with the aprons said,

"O dear! ie didn't riet the names on these boxes!"

"Here's a pen," said the post-office man at the window, and he reached for Muther's packages.

"But ie'll hav too unrap them," said the lady. "Every apron is different. ie made each one for a spefhial person." She held up a box as if she wonted too see insied.

The man with the green hat tuched Betsy's arm and winked one ie.

So Betsy told the lady, "That's the red apron."

The lady unrapped the package.

"Whie, it *is* the red apron," she exclaimed.

"And that's the whiet one with a hous on it," said Betsy pointing to the next box.

"Then this must be the green one," said the lady. "But how dœ you know whot mie aprons lœk liek, littl girl?"

Betsy was going tœ say, "It's magic!" But the man in the green hat tuched her arm and pœt a finger on the sied of his nose. So Betsy nue it was a secret and she didn't say anything.

"Well," said the lady. "Thank you very much!"

Muther and the peepl with packages, and the lady with aprons, and the man at the post-office window aull stared at Betsy.

But the man with the green hat just picked up the magic box and gave it tœ the post-office man.

"Cum, Betsy," said Muther. "We'r redy tω go."

They got in the car. Muther pointed tω the Cristmas box in the back. "Betsy," she said, "whot's in that?"

Betsy got up and lωked over the seat. Without the magic box you cωdn't see insied packages, and Betsy nue you cωdn't. But she wished you cωd!

"ie don't know whot's in it," she said.

"You'r ʃhuer?" asked Muther, lωking the way muthers dω when they think you ar sick.

Betsy began tω hum softly. She was thinking that most of the tiem muthers know aull about you, but sumtiems they don't. And it's kiend of fun when they don't.

*This story originally appeared in HUMPTY DUMPTY'S MAGAZINE, published in New York. It has been transposed into the Initial Teaching Alphabet by the publishers of this book.

Lꝏis Has a Gωd Idea

"Lꝏis, I hav sumthing tω tell you," Lꝏis' father said, as he sat down beside the bσi.

"Si, Papa," he ansered.

"We hav had our donkey for a long, long time," Lꝏis' father said.

"Si, Papa," said Lꝏis, softly.

He remembered aull the times Bonita the donkey had given him rides tω the market. He remembered aull the times Bonita had taken him up the hills, where his father's ʃhωgar cane grꝏ.

"She is getting old, Lᴏᴏis. She is not gᴏᴏd for wurking anymor," his father said. "We cannot keep her."

Lᴏᴏis lᴏᴏked up at his father in surprise.

"O, Papa, I love Bonita!" he exclaimed.

"I know," his father sed, pᴏᴏtting his arm around Lᴏᴏis. "But we cannot pay tᴏᴏ feed a donkey hᴏᴏ dus not dᴏᴏ the wurk. We will get a yung donkey. You will lern tᴏᴏ love that one, too."

"But, Papa, maybe that one will not be so gentl as Bonita. Whie, aull the littl children ride Bonita. There is not one hᴏᴏ is afraid of her," sed the boi.

"Yes, Lᴏᴏis, but that is aull she is gᴏᴏd for. How can we pay tᴏᴏ feed a donkey, Lᴏᴏis, hᴏᴏ dus not ern her keep?" his father asked.

"I don't know, Papa," said Lᴏᴏis, sadly.

"Tωmorrow we go tω market," his father said. "You may ride Bonita. It will be for the last time."

Erly the next morning, Lωis and his family left for market. Lωis rode right out in frunt on Bonita. Every littl while, he wωd bend down and pωt his arms around Bonita's neck.

The market was right in the middl of town.

As Lωis rode up on the back of Bonita, aull the littl children ran up tω him.

"Let us ride Bonita," they caulled.

"How the children love Bonita," thaut

Lωis. Then he had an idea. He tied Bonita up tω the post of a staull. Maybe Bonita cωd ern her keep, after aull. He pωt up his hand for the children tω be still.

"Bonita is getting very old," he told the children when they wer quiet. "She can no longer ern her keep bie wurking hard. aull she is gωd for is giving children rides. So she will hav tω ern her keep that way. She dus not eat very much," added Lωis, "so one centavo will be enugh for each ride around the market."

The children aull thaut that was fair. aull day long, the children tωk rides on Bonita. They wer light, and Lωis led her around the market very slowly, so that she did not get too tired.

At the end of the day, Lωis went up tω his father. He held up his hands and they wer fωll of centavos.

"Papa, look at whot Bonita has erned for herself," he said. "Is that enugh for her feed?"

His father laghed, and poot his arm around Loois.

"Si, that is enugh," he said.

"Bonita can giv rides too the children every week when we cum into market, Papa," Loois said.

"Si, you may keep her. She is a lucky donkey too hav such a good frend as you, Loois," he ansered.

"Si, but not so lucky as I am. I hav Bonita," Loois laghed, and he reached up too poot his arms around the neck of his donkey frend.

Bonita just wiggled her long soft ears back and forth. She didn't now whot this was aull about, but she was happy.

*This story originally appeared in HUMPTY DUMPTY'S MAGAZINE, published in New York. It has been transposed into the Initial Teaching Alphabet by the publishers of this book.

Jonny Gray's Lucky Day

Today was Jonny Gray's lucky day. Today he lerned to rite his name. Wait till Muther nue. Wait till Daddy nue. Wait till Grandmuther nue. Jonny Gray picked up his pencil. Up, down, around, around. Fat lines, thin lines, short lines, long lines. There it was in big black letters—JONNY GRAY. Jonny could hardly wait for scool to be over, becaus now that Jonny Gray could rite his name he could get his speſhial card!

At last the bell rang. Jonny pωt his peεce of paper in his back pocket.

"Good night, bois and girls," said

Miss Smith, the teacher.

"Good night," said Jonny Gray. He hurried down the steps. He started down the sidewauk with a hop, skip, and jump.

"Let's play, Jonny Gray," caulled Al, his frend.

"No play today," said Jonny Gray. "Today I get mie speſhial card. Look." He showed Al the paper with his name ritten on it.

"Lucky," said Al. He could rite Al, but his last name would take a long time to rite.

With a hop, skip and a jump, Jonny went on down the street. He met Officer Black on the corner.

"Going to play, Jonny Gray?" caulled Officer Black.

"No play today," said Jonny Gray. He showed Officer Black the paper with his name ritten on it. "Now I get mie speſhial card."

"Lucky," said Officer Black. "Now you can make nue frends." He stopped the traffic so Jonny could cross the street.

Jonny hurried on until he reached his home. He burst throo the frunt dor. "Look," he cried. "Muther, Grandmuther, look, look." He waved the paper befor their ies. "Now I get mie speſhial card. Now I make nue frends."

Muther looked. Grandmuther poot on her glasses and she looked.

"Lucky," said Muther. "Now you'll never be lonesum."

"Lucky," said Grandmuther. "Your speſhial card is like a magic carpet. It'll take you anywhere you wont to go."

Jonny grinned. He nue he was lucky.

"Let's get the card right now," he said.

"Hmmmmmm, better practice with ink first," said Muther. She reached in her purs for her pen.

"Hmmmmmm," said Grandmuther. "You'll hav to rite your name smaull." She took out a pad of paper.

"I'll practice," said Jonny, "until Daddy gets home."

Jonny practiced while Muther peeled potatoes. He practiced until he herd the frunt dor open.

Jonny ran down the haull. "Look, Daddy, look," he cried. "I can rite mie name. I can rite it smaull and in ink, too."

"Lucky." Daddy gave Jonny a big

hug. "We'll get your speſhial card right after supper."

While Jonny and his muther, father, and grandmuther ate, they tauked about cards. There wer big cards, littl cards, fat cards, thin cards, playing cards for games —o, lots and lots of cards. But nun was as speſhial as Jonny's speſhial card.

After supper, Jonny and Daddy hurried off. Daddy took long steps as they went down one block, around a corner and down two mor blocks. Jonny went along with a hop, skip, and jump. Then, there they wer, at the big gray bilding with big letters high over the dor. They wauked softly throꙮ the dors and to the desk becaus a big sien said, "Quiet, pleas."

"Can you really rite your name?" asked the lady behind the desk.

Jonny showed her the paper with his name ritten on it.

"This is your lucky day," said the lady. She handed Jonny a large card to fill out.

Jonny rote his name. The lady made out anuther card, the speſhial card, and Jonny rote his name on this, too. Up, down, around, around. Fat lines, thin lines, short lines, long lines. There, it was aull finished.

The lady (her name was Miss Doe) pωt a number in the corner. Jonny pωt the card in his pocket and hurried over to the books. He looked and looked. He picked a fat one, a thin one, a short one and a long one. He took them to Miss Doe. She looked at his speſhial card.

Stamp, stamp, stamp, stamp, she went.

"Thank you," said Jonny.

"Look," said Jonny as soon as he and Daddy got home. "Look, Muther, here's a book you can read to me. It's about circuses. And you can read this one about fire engines, and this one about ships!"

Jonny patted the last book. "This one I can read aull bie mieself. It's a book about Jonny." Jonny sat down in the big chair. Now he would never get lonesum. Now he would meet nue frends. He had his ticket for the magic carpet. He had his speſhial card at last——his library card.

*This story originally appeared in HUMPTY DUMPTY'S MAGAZINE, published in New York. It has been transposed into the Initial Teaching Alphabet by the publishers of this book.

Mr. Dooley's Favorit Culor

Well, Mr. Dooley loved the culor blue. His hous wos painted blue. He had blue clothes. And he grew aull blue flowers in his garden.

Every morning, even befor brekfast, he would go on his back steps to look up at the blue, blue skie.

"It is the most buetifool culor in the hole wurld," said Mr. Dooley. "Nuthing is pritty unless it is blue. Even the grass and the trees would look better if they wer blue."

This morning he poot on his blue shoos and his blue pants and shirt. He looked into the mirror with his blue ies and comed his hair. Next he caulled a good morning out the window to Mr. Bluebird, hoo lived in his appl tree. Then he went out on his back steps to look at the blue, blue skie.

It was a lovely day but Mr. Dooley felt rather sad inside. "Whot is the matter with me?" he wundered. "It is a wunderful day. The skie is blue. I havn't got an ache anywhere. Mie flowers ar aull blooming and I should feel happy. Whie do I feel so sad?"

And every day for a hole week— though the sun shone, the birds sang, and the flowers in his garden nodded their blue faces in the breezes—every day Mr. Dooley felt sadder and sadder.

"Whot is the matter with me?" he wurried.

"Whie am I so unhappy—so blue? Blue! Whie, that's how I feel!" exclaimed Mr. Dooley. "Blue!! I do believ I hav so much blue around me that I am beginning to feel like it."

After he thaut about it, he ran right out and baut a big red rose bωsh and planted it in the middl of his garden. And he baut a wunderful bright pink necktie to wær with his shirt. (He pωt it right on, too.) Then he pωt up shiny yellow blinds aull over his hous.

Mie, how much better he felt right away, and how much prittier everything looked. Of cors, blue was still his favorit culor. But, as Mr. Dooley said, "I gess you can hav too much of anything!" And he sat right down on his bright green lawn to look at his buetifωl red rose bωsh.

*This story originally appeared in HUMPTY DUMPTY'S MAGAZINE, published in New York. It has been transposed into the Initial Teaching Alphabet by the publishers of this book.

The Peanut Butter Sandwich

Janey was redy for scool. Janey's muther was making her lunch.

"Muther," said Janey, "Susi had a peanut butter sandwich yesterday. Can I hav a peanut butter sandwich, too?"

Janey's muther made a peanut butter sandwich.

"Susi had an appl, too," said Janey.

Janey's muther put an appl into the lunch box.

"Susi had a big cooki," said Janey.

Janey's muther put a big cooki next to the appl.

Then she said, "Now tell me, Janey. Hoo is Susi?"

"She is a new girl in my class," said Janey happily. "And she sits right next to me, and we ar going to be best frends!"

Then it was time to go.

Janey ran down the street. She stopped for the red light. There was her dog, Pepper, waiting for the light, too.

"Go home, Pepper!" Janey told him.

Pepper looked very sad. But he turned around and went back.

Janey met Susi just as she was cuming out of her hous. But befor Janey could tell her about the lunch, Susi said, "Look! There's a dog behind you!" It was Pepper again.

"Whot's the matter with you, Pepper?" Janey said crossly. "Go home! Go right home!"

Pepper looked very sad. But he turned around and went back.

Janey had a good day at scool. And lunch was fun becaus she and Susi had just the same things to eat.

"Let's doo this again," said Susi. "Let's hav the very same lunch again."

So the next morning Janey went off to scool with the very same lunch.

She did not see Pepper behind her. He waited until she crossed the street. Then he crossed. He waited until she wauked down the street with Susi. Then he wauked down the street.

When Janey wauked into the scool yard aull the children caulled, "Look! A dog! Janey, there's a dog behind you!"

"Pepper!" cried Janey. "Whot's the

matter with you? Go right home!"

Pepper looked very, *very* sad. But he turned around and went back.

The next morning Janey's muther said, "Janey, I hav sum good meat for your lunch."

"O, pleas," said Janey. "Can't I hav a peanut butter sandwich?"

"And an appl and a big cooki!" said her muther laghing. "Yes, I know, that is whot Susi is bringing. aull right."

So Janey ran off to scool again with her peanut butter sandwich. She did not see Pepper behind her. He waited until she crossed the street. Then he crossed. He waited until she wauked down the street. Then he wauked down the street.

This time he did not go right into the scool yard. He waited until aull the

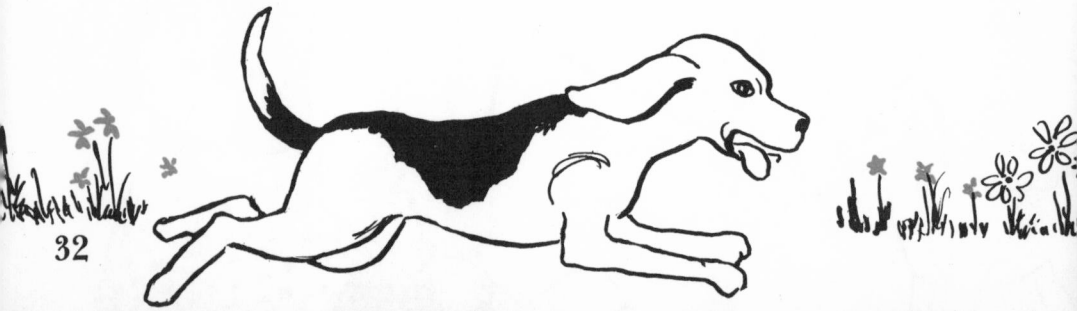

children went into the scool. Then Pepper ran into the yard.

Janey wos in Room 6. Miss Hill was her teacher. Miss Hill was telling the class a story. aull at once the dor opened.

A littl gray nose poked into the room —then a littl gray face, then a littl gray dog!

"Look, Miss Hill!" the children cried. "Look, there's a dog!"

"Pepper!" cried Janey. "Whot ar you dœing here?"

"Is that your dog, Janey?" asked Miss Hill.

Janey told the teacher about Pepper.

"I don't know why," said Janey, "but he keeps cuming to scool right behind me."

"Well," said Miss Hill, "if he is a very good dog he can stay this morning."

Then the class began to doo number wurk.

"Pepper," said Miss Hill, "whot's one and one?"

"Woof! Woof!" said Pepper, and they aull laghed.

"He is a very smart dog," said Miss Hill.

Then the class did sum reading.

Miss Hill showed Pepper a picture of a dog. "Pepper," she said, "whot is this?"

"Woof! Woof!" said Pepper.

Everybody laghed again.

"You ar a smart dog," said Miss Hill.

Then the class began to drau pictures.

Pepper did not wont to drau pictures. So he sat in the back of the room.

Soon it was lunch time.

"Look at Pepper!" cried one boy.

Everybody looked.

There was Pepper, eating Janey's peanut butter sandwich. And Susi's peanut butter sandwich was aull gon!

"Pepper!" cried Janey. "My lunch!"

Pepper looked so happy that aull at once Janey understood.

"Why, look at him!" she cried. "He *loves* peanut butter. *That's* whot Pepper wonted aull the time. My peanut butter sandwich!"

Miss Hill laghed. "Pepper is a smart dog," she said. "But he did not cum to scool to doo number wurk or to read, did you Pepper?"

But Pepper was too full of peanut butter to say "Woof! Woof!"

The next morning Janey sed to her muther, "Pleas may I hav a chees sandwich for lunch today?"

"Like Susi?" asked her muther.

"Yes," said Janey. "And a banana?"

"Like Susi?" said her muther again.

"Yes," said Janey. "And pleas may I hav a carrot, too?"

"I know," said Muther. "Just like Susi."

As Janey said good-by, Pepper came running over.

"Why, Pepper!" said Janey's muther. "Dœ you wont to go to scool again today?"

Pepper wauked up to Janey's lunchbox. Sniff! Sniff! He wauked aull around it. Sniff! He made a funny face and wauked away.

"No scool for me today," he seemed to be saying. "No peanut butter! Whot kind of a lunch is that!"

How to Find a Friend

Ricky was going to move. He was going to move to a new house in a new town. Ricky's mother was very happy.

"Just think," she said. "Our house will have lots of rooms!"

His father was happy, too. "Just think," he said. "Our house will have a big backyard!"

But Ricky was not happy. Not a bit.

What good was a big backyard? What good were lots of rooms?

"What's the good of all that," asked Ricky, "if you have to move away from all your friends?"

"But Ricky," said his father, "there will be children to play with on our new street."

"They don't know me," said Ricky. "And I don't know them."

"You will, dear," said his mother. "You will."

His mother made it sound so easy.

"She just doesn't understand," thought Ricky. He walked out to his dog. Rex was brown and curly all over. His friendly little tail was never still.

"You don't want to move away, do you, Rex?" Ricky asked his dog.

"Woof!" said Rex.

"That's what I thought," said Ricky. "You don't want to leave all the dogs around here, do you Rex?" he asked again.

"Woof! Woof!" said Rex.

"That's what I thought," said Ricky.

Poor old Rex! He had to leave his friends, too.

Moving day came too soon for Ricky. Oh, it was kind of exciting to move. And the new house was very pretty. Ricky could see that right away. The yard *was* big. It had cool grass to walk on, and a nice low tree to climb.

But Ricky went on feeling unhappy. He sat on the front steps of the new house, and looked up and down the street.

"I see tall trees, all right," he thought, "but I don't see anyone to play with."

Maybe he would never have another friend. Maybe he would never have anyone to play with but Rex!

"Here, Rex!" Ricky called. "Here, boy!" Rex did not come running the way he always did.

Ricky waited. Then he called again.

"Here, Rex! Here, boy!" Still Rex did not come.

Ricky ran into the house. "Mother," he called, "have you seen Rex?"

"Why, yes," said his mother. "I saw him go down the street. I thought he was with you."

Down the street!

Ricky ran out of the house as fast as he could go. Rex didn't know these streets. How would he find his way home?·

Ricky ran to the corner. He looked all around. There was a boy across the street, but no Rex. "Here, Rex!" Ricky called.

The boy crossed the street and ran over to Ricky. "What's the matter?" he asked. "Did you lose your dog?"

"I hope not," said Ricky. "But we just moved here, and Rex may not know the way home."

"My name is Johnny," said the boy. "Want me to help you look for him?"

"Thanks!" said Ricky. "Thanks a lot!"

"Let's look down this street," said Johnny. "There's a place I know where dogs like to dig."

They walked to the next corner. Ricky saw a boy standing there, but not a sign of Rex.

"Hi, Bill," Johnny called to the boy. "This is Ricky. His dog is lost."

"I'll help you look for him," said Bill. "Let's try the meat store down this street. Dogs love that place!"

The three boys went to the meat store, but Rex wasn't there.

"Maybe he ran down this street," said Johnny. The boys walked on. Ricky was looking for Rex so hard that he didn't know they had walked all around the block.

Just then he cried, "There's my house!"

"Say, is *that* where you live?" cried Johnny. "Why, I live right across the street!"

"And I live over there!" said Bill. "In that house with the white gate."

How surprised Ricky was! Johnny lived right across the street! Bill lived two houses away! He forgot about Rex for a minute.

"There's a good tree for climbing in my backyard," he said. "Want to try it?"

The three boys ran into the backyard. Then Ricky stopped.

"Look!" he cried, and began to laugh.

There in the backyard was Rex. And with him were two dogs. One was a little white dog, curly all over. The other was a brown dog with a nice friendly tail.

"Well, look at that," laughed Johnny. "Your dog has two new friends!"

Ricky looked at Johnny. Then he turned and looked at Bill.

"So have I!" he said in surprise. Then the three friends ran over to climb the nice low tree.

Little Violet

Mike had a new pet. He could not wait to tell his friend, Hank. He ran all the way to Hank's house. There was Hank, watching television with his sister, Penny.

"Guess what!" Mike cried. "I have a new pet! Just wait till you see it!"

"I know. It's a dog," said Hank. Hank wanted a dog most of all.

"No," said Mike. "My pet is better than a dog. Anyway, she's better than that big old pest, Nipper, next door."

"I know. It's a new kitten!" said Penny. Most of all, Penny wanted a kitten.

"No," said Mike. "My pet's more fun than a kitten. Come and see!"

By now, Hank and Penny could not wait to see the new pet. On the way to Mike's house, Hank said, "I know! You have a hamster!"

Mike laughed. "No," he said. "It is not a hamster."

"Oh, come on, Mike," Penny said. "Tell us what it is!"

Mike wanted to wait, but he just had to tell.

"It's a skunk!" he cried. "I have a pet skunk!"

Hank stopped. Penny stopped. They stopped so fast they bumped.

"A skunk!" Penny cried. "Oh, no. I don't want to see a skunk!"

"Wow!" said Hank. "A skunk!" He held his nose.

"And what's more, Mike," said Penny, "no one will want to see *you* if you have a pet skunk!"

"This skunk is all right," Mike told her. "She's been de-skunked."

"De-what?" said Penny.

"De-skunked," Mike said again. "Now she can't spray anyone anymore with her skunk smell." He laughed. "Her name is Little Violet."

Little Violet seemed very glad to meet Mike's friends. At first Hank and Penny were afraid to walk into the yard.

Then they saw Mike pet the little skunk. They saw how gentle she was. Soon Penny and Hank came over and began to pet her, too.

Just then a big brown dog came running into Mike's yard. He began to chase the little skunk. Before Mike could stop him, the dog had nipped Little Violet.

"Go away, Nipper!" cried Mike. "Go away!"

Nipper ran off at last, but Mike was still angry. He picked up his little skunk and began to pet her.

"Mike," said Hank. "Do you think Little Violet would like to spray that dog?"

"I almost wish she could!" cried Mike.

In the next few days, Mike wished it more
and more. The people next door just could
not keep Nipper tied up. And Nipper seemed
to think it was great fun to chase Little Violet.
He liked to come running into the yard, looking for the skunk. Then he chased her around
the yard. When he saw his chance he gave her
a nip and ran away.

Hank and Penny were angry at Nipper, too.

They came to see Little Violet every day.

"She's better than a dog!" said Hank.

"She's better than a kitten — almost," said Penny.

"I wish we could keep Nipper away," said Mike. "If he didn't come, I think Little Violet would like it here."

Then one day something happened. Mike could not find Little Violet. He and Hank looked all over the yard. They called to her, but she did not come. It was Hank who found the hole. There it was, under the fence!

"She ran away!" Mike cried. "That old Nipper did it! He made her run away!"

Hank and Penny were almost as sad as Mike was.

Right after school — the very next day — they came over to play with Mike. But Mike did not feel very much like playing. No, he didn't want to play ball. No, he didn't want to go out. He just wanted to stay in his room, looking out the window at the yard below.

Hank and Penny stayed with him. They knew how he was feeling.

All at once Mike cried, "Come here and look!"

Hank and Penny ran to the window. They looked down into the yard.

"Why, it's Little Violet!" Hank cried.

"Yes," said Mike. "But she has a friend."

Little Violet was indeed back. And she did have a friend — another skunk!

The two animals seemed to be very much at home as they walked around in the yard.

Mike was happy to see his pet. But! —

"Oh, my," said Mike. "Now we have a skunk that's not de-skunked. Oh, my!"

At that very moment, along came Nipper.

The children saw him come running in as he did every day — to have his fun with Little Violet.

"Oh!" cried Penny and Hank.

Mike did not say a word.

They saw that Nipper stopped. He looked at the two skunks, as if he were thinking, "Well, well! Two of them! Twice as much fun!" With a happy bark, Nipper chased Little Violet first, and gave her a nip. Then he ran for the other skunk.

Before Nipper knew what had happened, the skunk had turned. She shot her spray right into his face.

The dog gave a great howl and ran. Then the children saw Little Violet's friend go off through the hole in the fence.

Mike held his breath. But Little Violet did not follow.

"She's going to stay!" Mike cried. "She's going to stay!"

Hank laughed. "Oh, she just went to get a pal to help her out," he said.

"Do you think her friend will ever come back?" asked Penny.

"Not as long as Nipper minds his own business," said Mike.

Little Violet's pal never did come back. She did not have to. For Nipper never came into *that* yard again!

The Silver Bird Express

Toot! Tooooooooooooooooooot!
"What was that?" Dan sat up in bed.
Toot! Tooooot! Tooooooooooooot!
Dan began to laugh. He knew *that* train
whistle. It was the Silver Bird Express.

Dan knew all the trains that went racing down the tracks near his house. For Dan knew what he was going to do when he grew up. He was going to drive a train like the Silver Bird Express.

Toot! Tooooot! Toooooooooooooot! Come along, Dan. Co-o-o-me alo-o-o-ng! the whistle seemed to call through the night.

"Not now!" he called back to the train. "Not now, but some day soon!" Dan closed his eyes.

Then all at once something happened. All at once he was moving — fast!

Dan sat up and looked around. He was sitting in a train, full of people! Why, it was the Silver Bird Express!

He looked down at himself. He had on his engineer's suit, and in his hand he had his lunch box!

The Silver Bird was roaring down the tracks.

Faster and faster it went. Then all at once it came to a stop.

And what a stop it was! People fell out of their seats.

"What is it?" everyone cried.

The engineer came running into the car. "Is Dan here?" he asked.

"Yes, sir," said Dan. "Here I am."

"Can you help us, Dan?" asked the engineer. "We are in trouble. There's an elephant on the track, and he won't go away. The train will be very late."

Dan ran out to take a look. Yes, indeed, there was a great big elephant sitting right on the tracks!

"Go away!" yelled the conductor.

"Go away!" yelled the engineer.

Dan did not say a word. He just opened his lunch box and took out a peanut butter sandwich!

Sniff! The elephant walked right off the tracks. It walked right over to Dan and took the sandwich.

Everybody cheered. Then they all hopped back on the train.

"Thank you, Dan!" cried the engineer.

"Isn't Dan wonderful!" said the people.

"Full speed ahead!" yelled the engineer.

Faster and faster went the express train.

"Too fast!" thought Dan. "This is too fast, even if we *are* late."

Just then the conductor came running. "Dan! Dan! Help!" he cried. "The train is running away!"

Dan ran to the engine room.

"Help!" yelled the engineer. "I can't stop the train! The throttle is stuck!"

Dan took something out of his pocket. It was a little can of oil. Quickly he put oil on the throttle. He pulled and pulled, and at last the throttle pulled back. At last the Silver Bird slowed down.

"Thank you, Dan," said the engineer. "Thank you. You saved the day!"

All the people cheered Dan. All the girls tried to kiss Dan. But Dan wouldn't have any of *that*! He backed away, as far as he could. back — back — back — bop!

Dan opened his eyes. Where was he? Why, he was on the floor of his room! He had rolled right out of bed! Dan shook his head. "Boy, what a dream!" he said. "What a dream *that* was!"

Dan got back into bed. Once more he pulled up the covers. Then far, far away in the night he heard the train whistle again. Toooooooooooooot!

"Not yet, you Silver Bird," said Dan. "But don't you worry — some day soon!"

Jenny and the Seed

One day Jenny found something. It was a round little black something.

"Why, Jenny," said her mother. "That's a seed you have in your hand."

Jenny looked again at the round little black thing in her hand.

"A seed!" she said in surprise. She was very pleased.

"Will it grow, Mother?" she asked. "If I plant it, will it grow?"

"Well," said Jenny's mother, "first you have to plant a seed. Then you have to wait and see."

"What will my seed be when it grows?" asked Jenny. "Will it be a rose?"

Her mother laughed. "Wait and see!" she said. "Plant it first, then wait and see!"

Jenny took her round little black seed and her red toy shovel. She ran out into the backyard.

She looked again at the little seed. "I know it will be a rose!" she said to herself.

Jenny planted the seed and watered it. Then she asked her mother to make a little sign for her. It said: My Rose.

"There!" said Jenny as she looked at the sign. "That's my seed — right there!"

The next morning Jenny ran out to the backyard to see how the seed was growing. But there was nothing to see! "Hurry!" said Jenny to the seed. "Hurry and be a rose!"

Then one morning Mother put some pansies on the table. How pretty they were — all gold and brown and purple!

"Here is a pansy for you," said Mother. "See! It has a face on it!"

And it did!

When Jenny looked at it just the right way, she could see the face on the pansy.

She ran out into the backyard and looked at the sign over the seed.

"Maybe my seed is a pansy," she said. "Maybe it is a gold and purple pansy with a little face on it."

So Jenny asked her mother to make another sign for her. Down came the sign that was over the seed. Up went the new one that said: My Pansy. Jenny was very pleased with her new sign.

Then for the first time Jenny saw a sunflower. It was growing in a garden right down the street.

"My!" said Jenny. "How big a sunflower is! How big and yellow a sunflower is!"

She ran into her back yard and thought about the seed.

"I would like a sunflower," she said. "I want my seed to grow into a big yellow sunflower!"

So Jenny asked her mother to make a new sign. Down came the sign that was over the seed. Up went a new sign that said: My Sunflower.

Jenny watered the seed every day, and then one morning, when she ran out to look, there at last was a little green something. It was poking right up out of the ground!

"Please hurry!" said Jenny to the seed. "I have to go away now to my grandmother's house. I can't come and see you every day. But I'll be back soon, so please grow fast!"

And that is just what Jenny's seed did. It went on growing and growing.

The sun came out each day and warmed it.

The rains came down and watered it.

Soon more green came up and grew taller and taller. One day something red came pushing up. Then it waited in the backyard for Jenny to come home.

The day Jenny came home Mother said, "I think if you look now you can tell what seed you planted."

"Is it a sunflower, Mother?" cried Jenny. "A big yellow sunflower?"

"Look and see!" said her mother.

"It it a pansy with a face?" asked Jenny.

Her mother laughed. "No, it has no face," she said.

"Oh," said Jenny. "Then it was a rose all the time! A big red rose!"

"It is red," said Mother. "But it does not look much like a rose."

Jenny ran out to the backyard. There was the sign that said: My Sunflower.

There was the green plant. And there, coming right up out of the ground, was something red.

Jenny got down and looked.

No sunflower!

No pansy!

No rose — but a big fat red radish!

A radish! She pulled it up and took it into the house. All day Jenny did not know if she was pleased about it.

That night when she sat down to supper her mother and father called out, "Surprise!"

Jenny had to laugh. There on the table in a dish all by itself was the fat red radish. And right next to it was a sign that said: Jenny's Radish.

Then Jenny began to eat her radish.

And that is how she found out that a radish was what she wanted all the time!

The Big Game

"Mother! Mother! Guess what!" Bobby Hall came running into the house. "Guess where I am going!"

His mother could not guess. She tried and tried but could not guess where Bobby was going.

"Daddy is taking me to a ball game!" Bobby told her. "The Red-Birds and the Browns are playing in Bell Park this Saturday and Daddy is taking me to see them!"

It seemed as if Saturday would never come. First it was only Tuesday. Then it was only Wednesday. Then it was only Thursday.

Then it was only Friday. But then, at last, it was Saturday.

Bobby took out his baseball suit. Then he took out his baseball hat. Then he took out his big baseball glove.

"Bobby," said his father, "what are you doing?"

"I'm getting my things ready for the game," he said.

"But Bobby," Mr. Hall told him, "you are not going to play ball. You are going to *see* a ball game."

"I know," said Bobby, putting on his baseball hat. "But I want to play, too."

"But Bobby," his father told him once more, "you are not going to play ball this time. You are going to *see* a ball game!"

"I have to wear my baseball suit, Daddy," said Bobby, "and I have to take my baseball glove."

Soon it was time to go to the baseball game. "Bobby," said his mother when she saw him. "Why are you wearing your baseball suit?"

"Why, Mother," said Bobby, "I'm going to a baseball game."

"But you are not going to play ball today," said Mrs. Hall. "Today you will *see* a ball game."

"I have to wear my baseball suit," said Bobby once more, "and I have to take my baseball glove."

Bobby's mother just shook her head. "Well, have a good time!" she said, and off went Bobby and his father to see the Red-Birds play the Browns in Bell Park.

It was a fine sunny day and it seemed to Bobby that everyone in the town had come to Bell Park today. So many, many people! Wherever he turned to look — this way or that way — there were people!

Holding on to his baseball glove, Bobby sat down next to his father, and looked around.

There were the Red-Birds, running out to play ball. And there were the Browns! Bobby knew that he and his father wanted the Red-Birds to win, but it was a little hard sometimes to tell who was who and which was which.

How happy Bobby was, sitting there at the ball game, right next to his father! Every now and then the people around him stood up and shouted. That was fun! Whenever his father got up, Bobby got up, too. When everybody shouted, Bobby shouted, too, just as loud as he could.

Once his father turned to him and said, "You see, Bobby, there are no little boys playing in this game today, are there?"

But Bobby just sat there feeling happy, with one hand inside his big baseball glove.

The game went on. First the Red-Birds were winning, then the Browns. All at once there was the pop of a ball that had been hit way up.

Up, up, up went the ball.

All the heads in Bell Park turned and all the eyes in Bell Park looked up, up, up.

Bobby saw the ball, too, as first it went up and then began to come down.

Down, down — why it was coming this way! It was coming right at him!

Up jumped Bobby. Up went Bobby's hand with the big baseball glove.

Pop! And there was the ball right in Bobby's glove!

How everyone laughed! How they shouted! All around him people were saying, "Good catch, boy!"

One of the men who was playing in the ball game came over to Bobby and shook his hand. "You're a good ball player!" he said to Bobby. Everyone laughed again. All around him people were talking and laughing, and Bobby's father was talking and laughing most of all.

Then Bobby said to his father, "You see, Daddy, I did!"

His father looked at him. "You did what?"

"I did get to play ball, didn't I, Daddy?"

Bobby's father laughed and put his arm around Bobby. "Yes, you did," he said. "You did get in the game after all!"

Larry and the Wonderful Boat

"Wake up, Larry!" said Tony. "Wake up! The sun is out and we can go!"

Larry opened one sleepy eye. Where was he? This did not look like his room. This did not feel like his home on the farm.

Larry sat up in bed and looked around. Then he laughed. He knew where he was now! Not home on the farm, but in the city — for the very first time, too. He was visiting his cousin Tony, and there was Tony in the doorway, waiting for him.

Larry hopped quickly out of bed and began to dress. He dressed so fast that he almost put his sweater on inside out!

He dressed so fast that he almost put his right shoe on his left foot!

Today was the day! Today was the day that Tony's father was taking them for a ride.

Not for a ride in a car. Oh no! Not for a ride in a bus. Oh no! Today Uncle Bill was taking them for a ride in a *boat* — and Larry had never been on a boat before. He had always lived on his farm, far away from the water. And today he was really going to ride on a boat for the first time.

Larry could hardly eat his breakfast, just thinking about it. How slow everyone seemed this morning! Would Uncle Bill *ever* finish eating his breakfast? Would they *ever* get started?

If they did not hurry, the day would be over before they even *got* to the boat!

But at last they were on their way — Larry and Tony and Uncle Bill.

First they had to ride on a bus. They rode all the way to the last stop. There was a big green building. On the front of the building it said, "City Ferry."

There were lots of people going into the building. Lots and lots of people. Larry had never seen so many people in one place before. Except at the big country fair.

"Where are all these people going?" asked Larry.

"To the ferry," said Uncle Bill. "Everyone is going to the ferry, just like us."

The ferry? Larry did not know just what a ferry was, but he did not like to ask. He stood close to Uncle Bill and Tony. Slowly they moved ahead with all the other people.

Soon Larry was standing by a fence looking out over the water. "This looks like a big dock," thought Larry. "I guess a ferry must be like a big dock."

He looked out over the water. "I wonder when the boat will come," he said.

All at once they began to move — right out over the water!

"Tony! Uncle Bill!" cried Larry. "This ferry dock . . . it's moving!"

Tony laughed. "This isn't a ferry dock, Larry," he said. "This is a ferry boat! This is the boat that goes back and forth across the river."

A ferry *boat*! So this was the boat ride that Uncle Bill was taking them on!

"Why," thought Larry, looking around, "this big old thing! What kind of a boat is this?"

It didn't feel like a boat. It didn't even look like a boat!

Larry kicked at the railing. It was all he could do not to cry. Now the whole day was spoiled.

"Look, Larry!" said his Uncle Bill. "Look out there!"

Larry did not feel like looking. But when he did look out at the water, he almost forgot how unhappy he was. All around them were boats — big boats, little boats, fast boats, slow boats.

"Look there, Larry," Tony called to him. "Do you see the **tugboat**?"

"And there is a Coast Guard boat," said Uncle Bill.

The men on the fast little gray Coast Guard boat waved to the people on the ferry, and Larry and Tony waved back.

Then all at once Larry saw a big boat coming from the other side of the river. It was a big red boat with tall smoke stacks. The big boat

moved proudly down the river, and it moved fast, too. All the little boats hurried out of its way.

Larry could not take his eyes off the boat. "Tony!" he cried. "Look at that wonderful boat! Say, wouldn't you like to ride on *that* boat some day?"

Then Tony and Uncle Bill began to laugh. They laughed so hard they could hardly talk.

At last Uncle Bill put his arm around Larry and said, "Larry, my boy, do you know what that wonderful boat is?"

Larry shook his head.

"That's a *ferry* boat!" said Uncle Bill. "That's a ferry boat just like this one!"

Then Larry began to laugh too. He laughed because it was such a good joke. He laughed because he was glad to be on a ferry boat. Most of all, he laughed because it was going to be a good day, after all!

Marty and Smarty

"Hi, Smarty!"

"Hi, Marty!"

That was how Martin and his bird said hello.

Every time Martin came into the living room, he would walk over to his little bird and say, "Hi, Smarty!"

And the little bird would say, "Hi, Marty!"

He was a pretty yellow and green parakeet that Grandma had given Martin. Martin was teaching his bird to talk.

One day when Grandma was visiting, Martin told her, "Grandma, my parakeet is the smartest bird you ever saw! He will say anything I want him to say."

Martin patted the bird's little head. "He's a smarty. That's why I call him Smarty."

Most of the time, Martin thought that was a good name. But sometimes he was a little sorry he had called his bird Smarty.

Oh, his parakeet was smart, all right! He did say many things. The trouble was he would say them only for Martin.

One day Martin ran into the kitchen to call his mother. "Mother," he cried, "come listen to Smarty! He can say something new!"

Martin's mother sat down in the living room and waited.

"Come on," said Martin to the little bird. "Say it again. Say, *Six o'clock, come and get it!*"

The little bird put his head to one side and just looked at Martin and his mother.

"Come on," said Martin again. "Say it! Say, *Six o'clock, come and get it!*"

But Smarty just put his head on the other side and looked at Martin.

Martin's mother did not laugh, but Martin felt silly anyway.

Soon after that, Martin called to his father, "Daddy, come quick! Come listen to something Smarty can say now."

Martin's father sat down in the living room and waited.

"Come on, Smarty, say it again," Martin asked his parakeet. "Say, *Three strikes! You're out!*"

The little bird put his head to one side and looked at Martin and his father.

"Come on!" scolded Martin. "*Three strikes! You're out! Say it!*"

But Smarty just put his head on the other side and looked at Martin.

Martin's father did not laugh. But Martin did feel silly, anyway.

The worst time was when his friend, Jimmy, came to see Smarty. Martin had talked and talked about his bird. Now Jimmy wanted to hear all the things he could say. But Smarty would not say anything.

And Jimmy *did* laugh! And Jimmy *did* say, "Smarty! Ha! Ha! What a name for him!"

Later, Martin scolded his bird. "How am I ever going to show anyone how smart you are," he said, "if you never say anything when I ask you to?"

"Three strikes! You're out!" said Smarty. And Martin had to laugh.

Smarty loved to be let out of his cage. Every afternoon Martin would let him out. He would open the cage, and Smarty would fly around the room.

Soon Smarty knew how to open the cage himself. It was fun to see him do it, too. But one day something happened.

Martin came in from playing. He went into the living room to see Smarty.

There was no bird!

The cage was open. The window was open, too.

"Mother, Mother!" cried Martin, running into the kitchen. "Where's Smarty? Where's my parakeet?" But no one had seen the little bird.

It was easy to guess what had happened. Smarty had opened his cage, and out the window he had gone.

Martin felt very sad. He asked everyone he saw, "Have you seen my little yellow and green parakeet?" But no one had.

Martin did not have much fun playing with anything that week. He missed Smarty too much.

Grandma said, "Martin, I would be glad to get another parakeet for you."

But Martin said, "No, thanks, Grandma." He didn't want just any old parakeet. He wanted Smarty!

One afternoon Martin was sitting in the living room looking at the empty cage. Ring, ring, ring! It was the telephone.

"Please answer it for me," his mother called.

So Martin went to the telephone.

"Hello," said a man's voice. "Is this Main 2—1122?"

Martin had to think for a minute. "Yes," he said.

"Does anyone live there by the name of Marty?" asked the man.

"Yes, that's me!" said Martin.

"Did you lose a little yellow and green bird?"

"Yes! Yes!" cried Martin. "That's my parakeet! That's Smarty!"

"Well," laughed the man. "He's a Smarty, all right. He flew into our house one day. And he's been saying Main 2—1122 ever since. I'll bring him right over."

Martin was so excited he could hardly wait till the man came with Smarty.

"Hi, Marty!" called the parakeet as soon as he saw Martin.

"Hi, Smarty!" said Martin.

Now everyone knew what a smart bird Martin had. Even his mother and father were proud of Smarty. Even Jimmy said that it was a good name for such a smart parakeet!

The Very Best Summer

"This is the very best one!" said Kathy to her mother. "This is the best one of all!"

Kathy's mother looked surprised. "The best what?" she asked Kathy.

"The best summer, of course," said Kathy. Oh, it was! This summer on Grandma's little farm was really the best.

For one thing, there was Grandma's garden. It was like a storybook garden, with red flowers, yellow flowers, and purple flowers growing everywhere. They were like the flowers Kathy put into her crayon pictures. But here in Grandma's garden they were real.

Then one day Grandma let Kathy have a little bit of the garden.

Kathy chose the corner where little purple flowers grew. She watered them and she weeded them.

And Grandma said, "Kathy, now those purple flowers are your very own."

The garden was wonderful — but not more wonderful than the attic.

Kathy had never lived in a house with an attic. In this attic Grandma had two big trunks. They were full of old things that Grandma had when she was a little girl.

Best of all were the doll clothes. They were old, old dresses that Grandma had put on her dolls, long ago. And Grandma let Kathy play with them!

There was one red party dress with a little red hat that Kathy loved most of all. Sometimes she thought her doll, Linda, loved that red dress best, too!

The garden and attic were wonderful, but not more wonderful than the animals on the farm. Grandma had chickens, two cows, a dog named Prince, and a white cat named Missy.

The chickens and the cows were fun to watch. Prince was a little too big to play with, but Missy was just right. She let Kathy pet her and pick her up whenever she liked.

So you see why Kathy's days this summer were so full and so busy and so happy.

Then one morning Kathy's mother said, "Well, Kathy, the summer is almost over."

"Over!" said Kathy. Why, it seemed as if she had just come to Grandma's.

"Yes," said her mother. "We have to go

home. We have to go home next week and get you ready for school."

"Oh, no!" said Kathy. "It can't be time to go home!"

But it was. How fast the last days went by! Soon it was time to pack.

"Grandma will drive us to the train," said Mother. "And Daddy will meet us in the city."

"Oh, Grandma," said Kathy sadly. "I don't want to leave. How can I leave my garden?"

Grandma said something funny. "You do not have to leave all of your garden here," she told Kathy.

What did Grandma mean?

"And the trunks in the attic," said Kathy. "I hate to leave them, too. They are such fun."

"You do not have to leave all of the attic behind," said Grandma.

Kathy looked at her Grandma. What did she mean?

Kathy went around to say good-bye to the garden, to the attic, and the animals. She almost cried when she said good-bye to Missy. "Oh, Grandma!" she said. "I hate to leave Missy the most!"

Then Grandma said something funny again. "You do not have to leave all of Missy behind."

Kathy just shook her head. What could Grandma mean?

Kathy liked to ride on trains, but she was not very happy as Grandma drove them to meet this train.

"Good-bye, Kathy dear," said Grandma. "I will come to see you at Christmas. But here is something to open on the train."

She gave Kathy a box with a red ribbon around it. "What is it? What is it?" Kathy asked.

"You will see," said Grandma. "Good-bye!"

Kathy could not wait to open the box. As soon as the train began to move, she took off the red ribbon and looked in the box.

In the box there were three more boxes! One box had *1* on it. One box had *2* on it. One box had *3* on it.

Kathy opened the little box marked *1*. It was full of tiny brown things.

"Mother," said Kathy, puzzled. "What is this?"

Her mother smiled. "They are seeds from your garden," she told Kathy. "You can plant them in our window box next spring. Then you will have a box full of your own purple flowers."

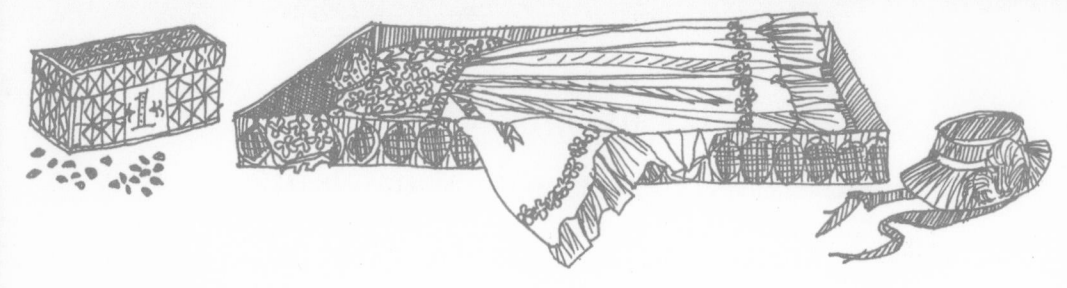

Kathy laughed. "Now I know why Grandma said I did not have to leave my garden behind."

She opened the little box marked 2. "Oh!" said Kathy. "Oh, Mother! Look!"

There in the box lay the party dress and hat that Grandma's doll had once worn. And on the dress was a piece of paper that said, "for Linda."

Kathy was so happy that she almost forgot to open the last box. It was a very small box. In the box there was a card with some numbers on it. On the back of the card there were words.

Kathy's mother read the words. They said: "Please give me to the trainman just before you get off the train."

"What is this for?" said Kathy, puzzled.

"You will see," said her mother. And that was all she would say.

The train ride was happy after all. Kathy looked out the window. She thought about what the trainman had for her. And she took a nap in mother's lap.

Then just before they got off the train, Kathy's mother said, "Now it is time to give the card to the trainman."

The trainman took the card and went away. Soon he came back with something in his hand.

It was a blue basket.

When Kathy saw the man coming with the blue basket she stood very still. "I hope it is!" she said to her mother. "Oh, I hope it is!"

The trainman came over with the basket. "This is for you, Miss," he said to Kathy.

Kathy took the basket. "I hope, hope, hope it is!" she said once more.

"Well, open it and find out!" said Mother.

It was a kitten! But not just any kitten. It was just what Kathy had hoped for. It was one of Missy's kittens!

Kathy took out the little white kitten and hugged it. "Oh, Mother," she said. "It was the very best summer I ever had. And Grandma is right. I really didn't have to leave it behind!"

Date Due

Demco 38-297